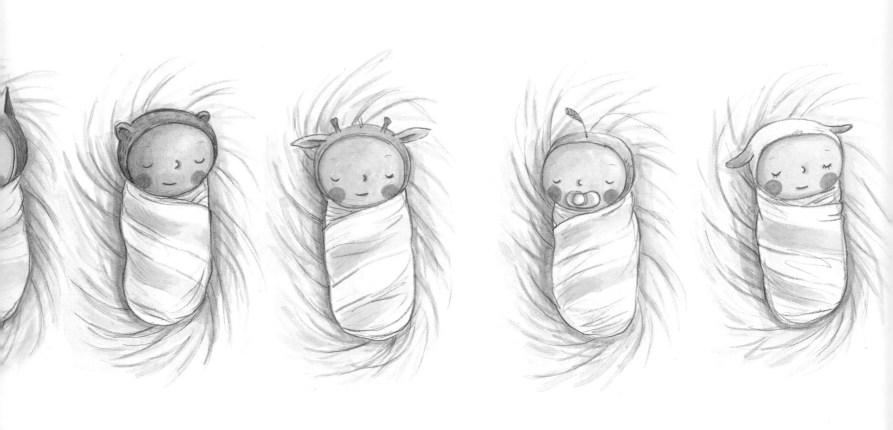

MARY LUNDQUIST

Cat & Bunny

BALZER + BRAY
An Imprint of HarperCollinsPublishers

Balzer + Bray is an imprint of HarperCollins Publishers.

Cat & Bunny
Copyright © 2015 by Mary Lundquist
All rights reserved. Manufactured in China.
No part of this book may be used or reproduced in any manner whatsoever without written permission except
in the case of brief quotations embodied in critical articles and reviews. For information address HarperCollins
Children's Books, a division of HarperCollins Publishers, 195 Broadway, New York, NY 10007.
www.harpercollinschildrens.com

ISBN 978-0-06-228780-9

The artist used pencil and watercolor on watercolor paper to create the illustrations for this book.
Typography by Dana Fritts
14 15 16 17 18   SCP   10 9 8 7 6 5 4 3 2 1

First Edition

For Jesse

Cat and Bunny were born on the same day, of the same month in the same year.

Right from the start, they did everything together. Just the two of them.

They daydreamed together.

They rode bikes together.

They had lunch together.

And they had lots of adventures together.

"Friends forever!" said Bunny.

"Just us!" said Cat.

Cat and Bunny's favorite game was the one
they had made up, called the Made-Up Game.
They played it every day and only they knew
the rules to it.

"Good move!" said Cat.
"Your turn!" said Bunny.

Then one day Quail asked,
"Can I play?"

Cat wasn't sure.
Bunny said, "Yes, of course!"

Soon all the children wanted to play.
Bunny said, "Of course!" to each one.

Cat didn't say anything.

Bunny was having too
much fun to notice . . .

when Cat ran away.

Cat sat all alone, waiting for Bunny
to find her. But Bunny didn't come.

Then she heard a purr and a rustle. It was a kitten!

She wasn't alone after all.

Soon Cat was playing a new
Made-Up Game with a new friend.

"Can I play, too?" asked Giraffe.

Cat thought for a moment. "Of course!" she said.

Once Cat showed Giraffe how to play
the new Made-Up Game, all the children
asked if they could join in.
Cat said, "Of course!" to each one.

The last to come was Bunny.

"Can I play the new Made-Up Game, too?" he asked.

Cat smiled and said . . .

"Of course!"